THE POMO

ELAINE LANDAU

THE POMO

Franklin Watts   New York   Chicago   London   Toronto   Sydney   A First Book

Map by Joe LeMonnier

Cover photograph copyright ©: National Museum of the
American Indian (#3450)

Photographs copyright ©: Lee Brumbaugh: pp. 3, 53, 54;
Ben Klaffke: pp. 8, 15, 20, 25, 26, 29, 30, 37, 38, 41, 42, 45; California
Department of Parks and Recreation: p. 13; Phoebe Hearst Museum of
Anthropology, University of California, Berkeley: p. 17; National Museum
of the American Indian: pp. 22 (#3450), 56 (#2241); The Smithsonian
Institution: pp. 33 (47749), 50 (75-14715); North Wind Picture Archives,
Alfred, Me.: p. 47.

Library of Congress Cataloging-in-Publication Data

Landau, Elaine.
The Pomos / by Elaine Landau.
p. cm. — (A First book)
Includes bibliographical references (p.) and index.
ISBN 0-531-20123-6 (hrd cover). — ISBN 0-531-15687-7 (trd pbk).
1. Pomo Indians — History — Juvenile literature. 2. Pomo Indians —
Social life and customs — Juvenile literature. [1. Pomo Indians. 2. Indians
of North America.] I. Title. II. Series.
E99.P65L36 1994
973'.04975 — dc20   93-23264 CIP AC

Copyright © 1994 by Elaine Landau
All rights reserved
Printed in the United States of America
6 5 4 3 2 1

CONTENTS

The Pomo: Indians of North Central California
9

Pomo Villages
12

Family Life
19

Food
24

Clothing
28

Trade
32

War
35

Crafts and Supplies
36

Religion
40

The Arrival of the Whites
44

Glossary
57

For Further Reading
59

Index
61

THE POMO

POMO FISHERMEN OF THE PAST WERE COMMONLY SEEN ON CLEAR LAKE (SHOWN ABOVE). THEY MADE STURDY BOATS FROM REEDS GROWING WILD IN THE AREA.

THE POMO: INDIANS OF NORTH CENTRAL CALIFORNIA

It was a good fishing season. California's Clear Lake teemed with blackfish, pike, carp, and bass. The Pomo Indians living nearby knew that the ample catch would help to ensure their survival throughout the coming winter months.

These Eastern Pomo Indians had built their village near the small streams that fed into the lake. During the *spawning* season, the fish swam into these shallow waters to lay their eggs. That enabled the Indians to catch a good amount of fish in a short time. After eating their fill, the extra was dried and stored for the winter.

This year, however, there was enough fish to trade with other Pomo groups, and several had been invited to the lake. There was much to do before

their arrival and everyone busily prepared for the visitors. They looked forward to a profitable and enjoyable trade. Their guests would be with them for several days — trading, feasting, gambling, and playing games.

Members of the visiting groups brought strings of beads to use in *bartering* for the fish. These beads were highly valued by the Pomos as they represented both wealth and status. After an agreed-upon number of beads was taken in return for the fish, the guests went home. All had done well in the exchange and none would go hungry that winter.

The Pomo Indians are native people who still occupy an area known today as north central California. Small bands of Pomos inhabited the Russian River valley, while other groups settled further north to Clear Lake and westward to the Pacific coast. The various groups — called Southern Pomo, Central Pomo, Northern Pomo, Eastern Pomo, Northeastern Pomo, Southeastern Pomo, and Southwestern Pomo (also known as Kashaya) — spoke seven different but related languages. And while the Pomos are very much alike in some ways, they are not identical. This book is about the Pomo Indians of California, how they lived and thrived before the Europeans arrived and their fate afterward.

POMO VILLAGES

The type of house as well as the village or community the Pomo Indians lived in depended largely on their location. Perhaps the harshest climate conditions were endured by the Pomos who lived near the Pacific Ocean. While summer temperatures might be well above 80°F (26°C), freezing winters were not uncommon. There was also a great deal of rain and fog throughout the year.

The Pomos inhabiting this coastal region usually established their permanent villages away from the beach. Other groups built their homes along the creeks that flowed into it. Often the larger villages were surrounded by smaller ones nearby.

During the warmer months, the Pomos also had temporary campsites closer to the ocean. The land along the beaches was backed by a dense redwood

THESE MAGNIFICENT CALIFORNIA REDWOODS ARE AMONG THE LARGEST TREES ANYWHERE IN THE WORLD. SOME GROW AS HIGH AS 275 FEET (84 M) TALL AND 12 FEET (3.7 M) WIDE.

forest. The Indians sometimes camped in the forest for short periods. But more often they came to the forest from their villages to gather food and useful materials. There were also temporary campsites near the salmon streams and in various other food-producing areas.

Still other Pomos lived farther inland, building their homes in an area filled with grassy valleys and rolling hills. The Russian River ran lengthwise through this region. These Indians experienced the most extreme weather conditions. Even though temperatures might reach 100° F (37°C) in the summer, a typical winter day was usually between 30° and 40° F (−1° to 4°C).

The Indians called the Eastern Pomos and Southeastern Pomos settled near Clear Lake — a body of water about 19 miles (31 km) long and up to 7 miles (11 km) wide in some places. The lake rests about 100 miles (160 km) north of what is now San Francisco.

Among the various Pomo groups, several types of structures were erected. The Indians living along the Pacific coast and near the redwood forests often built small, single-family structures of redwood bark slabs that stood from 6 to 8 feet (1.8 to 2.4 m) tall and ranged from 8 to 15 feet (2.4 to 4.5 m) long. Despite the lack of space, at times as many as a dozen

A POMO HOUSE NEAR CLEAR LAKE. THESE ROUND STRUCTURES MADE FROM BRANCHES, GRASS, OR REEDS DIFFERED FROM THE SMALL REDWOOD SLAB HOMES OF THE POMOS ALONG THE PACIFIC COAST.

people might live in one of these houses. In some places, the houses were surrounded by a fence made of brush. This enclosed area was useful for drying acorns — an important food source for the Pomos.

The Pomos living in the valleys farther inland along the Russian River as well as near Clear Lake generally built *communal* structures. These were houses shared by several families. The dwellings were usually round or L shaped and were made of grass, willow branches, or reeds known as *tules*, which the Indians took from the marshes surrounding Clear Lake.

In the Eastern and Southeastern Pomo homes, each family had its own fire as well as its own entrance. However, all the families shared the common storage space and a large central baking pit. These multifamily homes were usually about 200 yards (180 m) apart from others, and they spanned about 2 miles (3.2 km).

In addition to the communal houses, the villages often had several buildings for the group's use. One was a *sweathouse* — a small circular structure generally made of earth, reeds, and bark erected over a hole in the ground. The sweathouse door always faced south. Heated with steam produced by pouring water over hot stones, the village men and women entered it daily for sweat baths. Sweating was believed to produce a feeling of well-being as well as to purify the person for a religious experience.

A Pomo village usually also had a large meeting hall for dance ceremonies and various special events. It was an earth-covered lodge as large as 60 feet (18 m) wide for certain religious rituals.

THE INTERIOR OF A SOUTH-EASTERN POMO CEREMONIAL HOUSE. PART OF THE STRUCTURE IS BUILT UNDER-GROUND.

Each Pomo village was inhabited by one or more extended family or kin groups. A Pomo family usually consisted of about five to six members. Everyone had relatives close by, however, so a village might contain anywhere from one hundred to two thousand people.

In villages with more than one extended family, the different family heads or chiefs acted as a ruling council. Although each Pomo group or village was independent of the others, they sometimes banded together for important purposes. The Pomos frequently held trade feasts to obtain food or other highly valued materials. In times of war, they also united forces for a stronger defense.

Rank within the Pomo village was an important sign of status. An individual might be especially well thought of as a result of the wealth he acquired or his family's riches or background. Those with important positions within the group were also usually looked up to. The leaders or captains of a village were especially honored and respected by others. It was their responsibility to settle disputes and to see that everyone was properly taken care of. They also organized the village's activities, called for ceremonies, and welcomed guests. The captains were sometimes assisted by others in seeing that all went well.

FAMILY LIFE

Much of the activity in a village centered around closely knit family units. Marrying and having children were considered important events. It was crucial to ensure that the family continued. In some Pomo villages, marriages were arranged by the parents or family. The young people involved, however, had to agree to these matches.

In other groups, Pomo youths were free to pick their own partners. But while a young man or woman could not be forced to marry someone against his or her will, a son or daughter was also not permitted to select a person their parents disliked.

Once a choice was agreed upon, the groom moved into the bride's home for a time. That gave him a chance to get to know her family. At this point gifts were usually exchanged. In Northeastern Pomo villages, the boy's parents brought gifts for the girl's family. In Eastern and Southeastern groups, both families presented one another with gifts the morning after the boy moved in. A boy's parents might give valuable beads, while the girl's family usually offered beautifully made baskets. Foods such as acorn soup

A BOWL OF TAN ACORN SOUP. IN THE PAST, WHEN A POMO BOY AND GIRL WED, THIS SOUP AND OTHER FOODS WERE OFFERED AS GIFTS BETWEEN THEIR FAMILIES. WHILE THE INDIANS USED MANY TYPES OF ACORNS FOR FOOD, TAN ACORNS WERE KNOWN TO BE ESPECIALLY SWEET.

and items such as rabbit-skin blankets might also be exchanged between the newly united families.

After their stay in the bride's home, the young man and woman moved in with the groom's family. A feast was held and more presents were given. Among Eastern and Southern Pomos, the couple might move from one family's home to the other for a time.

Yet once a baby was expected, the couple usually stayed with the wife's family until the infant's birth. Depending on where space was available, the three then moved in with either the man or woman's family.

The birth of a child was special to the Pomos. A woman wishing to become pregnant might sit on a rock thought to be magical or drink from a special stream. While carrying the child she followed certain food, travel, and work restrictions. In Northeastern Pomo villages, babies were born in a shelter built specially for that purpose. The mother and infant would remain there for a few weeks following the infant's birth.

Among the Eastern Pomos babies were born in the mother's family's house. Females from the father's family, however, were also involved in the child's birth. The father's mother or sister would visit the house to bathe the baby in a special basket as well as help care for the infant.

BASKETS WOVEN BY POMO WOMEN SUCH AS THE ONE SHOWN HERE WERE USED AS BABY CARRIERS. THEY WERE USUALLY ABOUT 13 INCHES (33 CM) WIDE AND 22 INCHES (56 CM) LONG.

When the child turned one, he or she was named for a dead relative. It was believed that the child would grow up to be like the person. However, because names were thought of as private property, the child also had nicknames. Only the parents would actually address him or her by the real name.

Grandparents played an important role in a young person's upbringing. Usually several old people stayed close to the home tending the fire and the children. Their help allowed parents to hunt, fish, and gather food to feed the family.

While growing up, children were instructed in the ways of their people. Young boys learned tribal songs and at about twelve years of age were given a bow and arrows. As a young girl grew older she was taught basket weaving and how to gather and prepare food.

The Pomos observed special customs at death as well as at birth. A dying person was surrounded by his loved ones, who openly displayed their grief. Following his death, the body remained in the home for four days. Then it was burned along with gifts from friends and relatives. Most of the dead person's possessions were also burned, and sometimes his house was burned as well. A year after the death still more gifts were burned as an offering to the deceased.

FOOD

Like many native peoples, the Pomos largely lived off the land. Acorns were plentiful and the Indians gathered many different types to eat. The acorns were used to make bread and mush, which could be stored and eaten throughout the year. The Pomos also collected *buckeye* nuts, berries, and several types of healthful grasses, roots, and bulbs. Those near the seashore sometimes gathered dried seaweed and *kelp*, which were considered special treats.

Depending on where they lived, and on the season, Pomo men hunted for various types of game. Deer, elk, and antelope were sought out, although smaller animals such as rabbits and squirrels were eaten, too. Sometimes a hunter wearing a deer-head mask and robe would quietly venture into the woods

ACORNS WERE AN IMPORTANT FOOD SOURCE FOR THE POMOS AND OTHER INDIAN TRIBES IN THE REGION. ACORN DISHES ARE STILL PREPARED BY LOCAL NATIVE PEOPLE AT FALL ACORN FESTIVALS.

A POMO MAN MAKES A FISH TRAP SUCH AS THE ONES USED BY HIS ANCESTORS. THE INDIANS WOVE THESE TRAPS AND BROUGHT THEM ALONG WHEN THEY FISHED IN SHALLOW STREAMS OR ON LAKES IN THEIR BOATS.

with one or two others. Other times a fenced-in area made of brush was built to trap the animals. Hunters usually killed large game with bows and arrows or spears. Nets and traps fashioned from baskets were successfully used to snare smaller game.

The Pomos who lived near lakes, streams, or the ocean were excellent fishermen. Those near Clear Lake went stream fishing in the spring and fished and dug for clams in the lake during the summer. In the cooler months the Indians hunted *waterfowl*.

While some of the fishing, hunting, and gathering areas were shared by everyone, others were privately owned. Certain fruit-bearing trees and seed-producing land tracts were the private property of Pomo individuals or families. Such areas were solely for their owner's use.

CLOTHING

During the warmer months, Pomo men usually didn't wear clothes, although some Eastern and Southeastern Pomo males wore rabbit-skin *breechclouts*. In rainy or cooler weather, they wore mantles that tied around the neck and belted at the waist. Depending on the group's location, the mantles might be made of redwood, willow bark, or tule. Only very wealthy or important men had animal-skin *mantles*.

    Unlike the men, Pomo women always wore some type of skirt that covered their body from the waist to their ankles. They usually also wore mantles covering them from their necks to their waists. Like the men's mantles, the women's garments were generally made of whatever bark or reed was common to their area.

THE POMOS USED MARSH REEDS FOR MANY PURPOSES. IN ADDITION TO BEING FASHIONED INTO GARMENTS, THEY WERE USED IN THE CONSTRUCTION OF BOATS, HOUSES, AND FISH TRAPS.

THIS BEAUTIFUL HEADDRESS IS AN EXAMPLE OF OUTSTANDING POMO ARTISTRY. LIKE OTHER CALIFORNIA INDIANS, THE EARLY POMOS DID NOT WORK WITH GOLD OR SILVER. INSTEAD THEY USED SHELLS, BONE, SEEDS, FEATHERS, AND PRETTY STONES FOR ADORNMENT.

In cooler weather, women sometimes wore skirts made of animal skins beneath their bark or reed skirts.

For protection against the worst weather, both Pomo men and women used animal skin blankets. The Indians usually used whole skins, but also wove together skin strips to fashion good-sized blankets. The finished garments were draped across the person's shoulders and fastened in front. Rabbit-skin blankets were perhaps the most common, although coastal Pomos often made them from otter skin. Indians living farther inland also created wildcat-skin, gopher-skin, and bearskin blankets.

The Pomos didn't wear shoes most of the time. However, men who lived near Clear Lake's abundant tule marshes frequently wore moccasins and leggings woven from these reeds. It is also believed that some Pomos made deerskin boots to protect their feet from rocks and brush.

At special ceremonies, a number of Indians might be seen in beautifully crafted belts, neck bands, and wristbands made from brightly colored beads, shells, and feathers. Such articles reflected a person's wealth or position within the village.

TRADE

Trading goods with Pomo groups from other areas was common among these Indians. In this way the various villages could protect against famine or increase their wealth. When a village had a surplus of a desired item it called a trade feast. Other Pomo groups were invited to the village to exchange goods or beads for whatever their hosts had to offer.

    Clamshell beads were used as a form of money among the Pomos. These beads were difficult and time consuming to produce. First the clamshells either had to be secured through trade or collected from the ocean or bay. Then the shells were broken into small pieces and partially shaped before being drilled and strung. At that point, the rough beads were smoothed and rounded. Keeping his hands

A POMO MAN DRILLS BEADS. A FINISHED SET LIES NEXT TO HIM. EARLY POMOS USED STRUNG BEADS AS A FORM OF MONEY AT TRADE FEASTS.

moist, the bead maker would continuously rub the beads against a flat stone until they looked polished.

The more beads an individual had, the greater his wealth. Therefore these beads were readily traded for animal skins, food, salt, basket-making materials, bows and arrows, blades, animal traps, feathers, robes, belts, and other items.

Using the clamshell beads as a trade medium served as an important link between Pomos who lived far from one another and spoke different languages. Besides the elaborate village trade feasts, both individuals and small groups of Pomos often went on trading trips to other regions. They even established trade relationships with other tribes. In addition to the clamshell beads, the Pomos sometimes used "Indian gold" in trading. Indian gold wasn't actually gold, but 1 to 3 inch (2.5 to 7.5 cm) cylinder-shaped pieces of the mineral magnesite. The Pomos were quite advanced in developing a currency (money) system. Having devised a number system, they became known among native peoples as the "great counters."

WAR

To resist an outside threat, groups of Pomos banded together at times for battle. A war chief was elected to lead this effort. Wars were waged to stop theft of the village's supplies, poaching on their land, kidnapping Pomo women and children, or for other reasons. Before going to battle, special war dances were performed. The people prayed and made offerings. Everyone hoped for their people's success.

Ending hostilities was not always easy. Usually there were several visits between the victors and representatives from the defeated tribe to work out an acceptable surrender. Besides providing the winners with offerings, the losers also had to give something to the families of those killed in battle.

CRAFTS AND SUPPLIES

The Pomos were skilled at designing tools and weapons necessary for survival. Knife shafts were carved from rock and axes were fashioned by attaching handles to these blades. The Pomos near Clear Lake's marshes made boats of tule and used these reeds to create food mats, baby diapers and numerous other items.

In addition to making what they needed for everyday life, the Pomos were also extremely skilled at producing lovely items for ceremonies and special occasions. These included the beautiful ear ornaments worn by both men and women. The men's were made of wood and often were decorated with painted designs, beads, and feathers. The female ear orna-

SUSAN BILLY IS A WELL-KNOWN POMO BASKETMAKER
WHOSE WORK HAS BEEN HIGHLY ACCLAIMED.
HERE SHE'S PUT OUT SOME OF THE MATERIALS SHE
WILL NEED TO START A NEW BASKET.

THE EARLY POMOS DID NOT HAVE POTTERY, THEREFORE THEY USED DIFFERENT TYPES OF BASKETS, SUCH AS THIS INTERESTINGLY DESIGNED WILLOW BASKET, TO STORE AND CARRY THINGS.

ments tended to be more delicate and were fashioned from bird bones. They were sometimes adorned with small woven disks.

However, the Pomos were especially well known for their magnificent baskets. To collect materials for their basket work, Pomo women gathered sedge grass roots, bulrush roots, and willow and redbud branches. These beautifully decorated baskets were created in a broad range of weaves and shapes. Some were nearly as flat as plates while others were more rounded. These baskets might be completely covered with brilliantly colored feathers and an array of shells.

Splendid Pomo baskets were both given as special gifts and used in important ceremonies. These baskets were highly valued and regarded as a sign of wealth. People wanted to possess them just as they wanted the clamshell beads used in trading. Other less elaborate baskets were used for practical purposes.

RELIGION

Many spiritual aspects of Pomo life were overseen by religious healers or shamans. Shamans supervised important rites and ceremonies. There were several types of shamans or doctors among the Pomo Indians. These included those who specialized in time-honored tribal ceremonies, those who used herbs to cure illnesses, and two other types of healers known as singing, or outfit doctors and sucking doctors.

When called upon, a shaman was usually paid for his services with clamshell beads. Individuals needing a shaman were expected to pay whatever they could afford. Although at first these religious doctors were usually men, after 1870 there were reports of female healers among the Pomos after 1870.

POMO PRAYER ROCKS WERE CONSIDERED SACRED PLACES.

A POMO INDIAN MIGHT GRIND ACORNS ON THE GRINDING AREA OF A PRAYER ROCK HOPING TO BENEFIT FROM THE POWER OF THIS CHARMED STONE.

One of the important religious ceremonies practiced by a number of California Indian tribes besides the Pomos was the Kuksu cult. The Kuksu cult involved dancers impersonating, or acting as, a god or gods while conducting rituals to promote the village's well-being and its people's good health.

Kuksu dances were performed only by males. They danced and turned their bodies in circles to express their oneness with the universe. Often these dancers were clad in breastplates and headdresses decorated with woodpecker feathers. Many also carried painted staffs with feathered tips. Sick people hoping to be cured were brought up to the dancers. Afterward the performers went off into the woods, symbolically taking illness and sin from the village.

During the ceremony boys between ten and twelve years of age were initiated into a ghost society to which all Pomo adult males belonged. As members they were made familiar with the group's customs and the proper behavior expected of a Pomo man. In addition, a select number of males were tutored in the sacred ritual knowledge of their people and inducted, or accepted, into the secret Kuksu society.

THE ARRIVAL OF THE WHITES

The Pomo's existence dramatically changed with the arrival of the whites. By the 1700s, the Spanish were advancing northward through California. They established missions to *convert* the Indians, whom they regarded as "savages." By 1817, a mission at San Rafael actively sought Indian converts from as far north as Santa Rosa — located amid Southern Pomo villages. In the next few years, the missions penetrated deep into Indian country, extending their influence upon still more Pomo land.

    Lacking respect for the beliefs and lifestyles of their converts, the Spanish often dealt with the Indians brutally. They forced the Pomos to work at the missions and severely disciplined runaways. Punishments included using shackles and hobbles as

THIS SPANISH MISSION IS TYPICAL OF MANY BUILT THROUGHOUT CALIFORNIA. WHILE NEWLY CONVERTED NATIVE PEOPLE WERE PROMISED A PLACE IN PARADISE, THEY WERE CRUELLY TREATED ON EARTH. MANY WERE MADE TO DO HARD LABOR AND FORBIDDEN TO SPEAK THEIR LANGUAGE OR PRACTICE THEIR CUSTOMS.

well as imprisonment and floggings. When the free Pomos threatened to avenge the mistreatment of their people, the missionaries described them as harder to convert and control than other native peoples they had come across.

The Indians' plight worsened in 1822. Spain had granted Mexico its independence, and California was incorporated into the Mexican Republic. The Mexicans gave their own people land grants to establish ranches in South and Central Pomo territory. This expansion was backed by ruthless military actions throughout the region. The Pomos never knew when they would be captured and sold as slaves to develop the land stolen from them.

During the 1830s and 1840s, increasing numbers of Pomos were exterminated as a result of the Mexicans' deliberate campaigns to eliminate or enslave them. One such incident in 1841 involved a Mexican rancher named Salvador Vallejo. Vallejo had asked the Pomos to work on his property. When they refused, he called out a detachment of Mexican troops that massacred the village's men in their sweathouse.

Similar abuse of the Pomos later continued at the hands of American settlers. In 1847, two men named Charles Stone and Andrew Kelsey took over Vallejo's ranching and planting efforts. Their brutality toward the Eastern Pomos was infamous and eventually resulted in the two men's murder by the Indians.

Unfortunately, the death of Stone and Kelsey proved devastating for the Pomos. In 1850, the United States Cavalry arrived in Eastern and Southern Pomo country to avenge the two. Before

ALTHOUGH THE CAVALRY WAS SUPPOSED TO MAINTAIN LAW AND ORDER, THE NATIVE PEOPLE WERE NOT SEEN AS HAVING RIGHTS. OFTEN, PROTECTING THE WHITES CAME TO MEAN DRIVING OUT OR MASSACRING THE INDIANS.

leaving, they mowed down a group of Indians without warning who had been fishing on an island.

The cavalry's thirst for revenge, however, was still unquenched. The white soldiers continued westward, killing Northern and Central Pomo Indians who had nothing to do with Stone's and Kelsey's deaths.

In 1851, the United States government halfheartedly tried to bring about peace between the whites and the Indians. Colonel Redick McKee was sent to the area to both devise a treaty and establish a *reservation* for the Eastern and Southern Pomos. But as it turned out, McKee was ill equipped for the task. He knew little about Pomo customs, and his interpreter wasn't even familiar with Pomo languages. As a result, the document drawn up as a treaty never received Congressional approval and the reservation land was not set aside.

Instead, even larger numbers of American settlers flooded the region. Anti-Indian feelings ran high as many whites grew determined to erase any trace that the native people ever existed. Areas the Northeastern Pomos inhabited for years were no longer safe havens. In 1856, many of these Indians were captured and forced to live at the Indian Reserve near Fort Bragg and the Round Valley Reservation.

With the Indians out of the way, whites took over their land and had it officially deeded to them. Two years later the Indian Reserve was dissolved. That left large numbers of Northeastern Pomo with nowhere to live and no way to get their land back. To survive, many Pomos now had to bend to the white ranchers' demands. Some let the Indians live on their ranches in exchange for long hours of work with almost no pay.

Other Pomo groups continued to feel the sting of white settlements as well. The Eastern and Southeastern Pomos' traditional ways of survival were severely hindered by pioneers who forbade them to gather seeds and nuts on the land they claimed as their own. In any case, rich gathering areas had become scarcer as the settlers chopped down forests to build their homes.

The Pomos were further harmed by the smallpox, tuberculosis, and cholera *epidemics*, which largely devastated what was left of their population. Scores more died after being exposed to the whooping cough, measles, and various strains of the flu. While the whites quickly recovered from such illnesses, these diseases were unknown to the native people, who had no *immunity* against them.

Throughout north central California, diseases brought by the whites finished much of what the

A POMO WOMAN USES A WOVEN SEED BEATER TO GATHER NATURAL GRASS SEEDS. GATHERING SEEDS AND NUTS BECAME MORE DIFFICULT ONCE WHITE SETTLERS TOOK OVER THEIR LANDS.

bloody massacres and military campaigns against the Indians had set out to do. Between 1850 and 1871, the Pomo population was reduced to a fraction of its former size. It was difficult to effectively carry on the tribal customs and religious rituals with so many of their people gone. And in the face of widespread devastation, it sometimes seemed pointless to perform ceremonies for their people's well-being.

In 1872, however, the Pomos felt a glimmer of hope after news of a wonderful event occurring on a faraway Nevada reservation reached them. There an Indian prophet from another tribe had had a vision in which all native peoples had had their land and former way of life restored to them. He predicted that the white people would vanish and that the Indians they killed would return. Believers in the prophecy, or vision, took part in a ritual involving chants and dances known as the Ghost Dance.

Clinging to this dream, some Pomos tried to remain hopeful. They built a lodge in which to perform the Ghost Dance and continued these ceremonies for nearly two years. But when the predictions did not come true and the whites continued taking Pomo lands, many lost faith.

As time passed, the already dwindling Pomo population further declined. Eventually many of the remaining Pomos ended up on reservations and rancherias or government-owned parcels of land. Yet at times these resourceful people employed the whites' legal system to their advantage. For example, in the early 1900s, an Eastern Pomo man went to court and won the right to vote for Indians living off the reservations. In addition, by 1910 about one-half of all Northeastern Pomo children were attending school. And in the 1930s, the Pomos, working with other native peoples, put an end to the segregation of Indians and whites in schools and other facilities.

The Pomos also strove for reform in health care and living conditions. They petitioned the courts to secure a place to live for groups whose land had previously been seized. The Pomos often allied themselves with American Indian organizations hoping to improve their people's quality of life.

Unfortunately, in the 1960s the government abandoned, or "terminated," many of the rancherias' programs. This stopped even the meager funding these people had relied on. The land tracts were divided up and given to the Indian families inhabiting them. But the gift came with a bitter twist. As landowners, the Indians now had to pay property taxes. Those who couldn't raise the money lost the plots they'd lived on for years while whites took over the acreage.

POMO DANCERS IN TRADITIONAL COSTUMES PERFORM ANCIENT DANCES AT A FESTIVAL. DANCE, AN IMPORTANT PART OF INDIAN CULTURE, CONNECTS THE PAST TO THE PRESENT.

A POMO MAN SHOWS HOW A DANCE WHISTLE IS MADE. THESE INSTRUMENTS ARE STILL PLAYED AT TRADITIONAL CEREMONIES. SOME SOUND LIKE THE WIND, WHILE OTHERS SOUND LIKE BIRDS.

Some of the displaced Pomos moved to cities nearby and distant, as numerous Indians had done before them. Unfortunately, the family incomes of the Pomo often remained low. When they were able to find work it was frequently in poorly paying jobs, such as seasonal fruit picking or as household domestics.

Although both on and off the remaining reservations and rancherias some Pomos tried to keep the ways of their people alive, their native language was generally not spoken among them. Common staples of their present diet were often white bread and beans. Acorn mush and game were usually eaten only on special occasions.

Yet in more recent years an increasing number of Pomo Indians have gone to college and found places in the professional world. There has also been a renewed interest in the tribal customs and ceremonies of the past among young Pomos. In some areas, Pomos of all ages have turned to the songs and dances of the past as a vital link to their heritage. Pomos who are Catholic, Methodist, and Mormon have tried to incorporate the beliefs of their ancestors into their own religions.

Pomo basketmaking is still carried on by women who learned the art from their mothers and grand-

POMO BASKETS, SUCH AS THIS ONE, MAY BE DECORATED WITH SHELLS, BEADS, AND FEATHERS. THE POMOS ARE KNOWN FOR THEIR BASKETS — SOME SELL FOR HUNDREDS OF DOLLARS.

mothers. And family ties and relationships continue to be highly valued among these people. Perhaps some of the remaining Pomos may be able to combine the best of the old world with the new.

GLOSSARY

Bartering   trading

Breechclout   a piece of cloth worn (by men) around the hips and thighs

Buckeye   a type of horse chestnut growing in North America

Communal   shared or belonging to a community

Convert   to change from one religion or set of beliefs to another

Epidemic   a widespread disease affecting many people

Immunity   protection from a disease

Kelp   large coarse seaweeds

Mantle   a cloak without sleeves covering the upper body

Reservation   a tract of land set aside by the government for Indian use

Spawning   a fish laying its eggs

Sweathouse   a small circular structure built over a hole in the ground and heated with steam

Tule   a type of marsh-growing reed

Waterfowl   a waterbird or swimming game bird

FOR FURTHER READING

Avery, Susan, and Linda Skinner. *Extraordinary American Indians.* Chicago: Childrens Press, 1992.

Brown, Anne Ensign. *Monarchs of the Forest: The Story of the Redwoods.* New York: Dodd, Mead, 1984.

Dixon, Ann. *How Raven Brought Light to People.* New York: Macmillan, 1992.

Freedman, Russell. *An Indian Winter.* New York: Holiday House, 1992.

Goble, Paul. *Love Flute.* New York: Bradbury, 1992.

Lavitt, Edward, and Robert E. McDowell. *Nihancan's Feast of Beaver: Animal Tales of the North American Indians.* Santa Fe, N.M.: Museum of New Mexico, 1990.

Newman, Sandra Corrie. *Indian Basket Weaving; How to Weave Pomo, Yurok, Pima, and Navajo Baskets.* Flagstaff, Ariz.: Northland Press, 1974.

Shemie, Bonnie. *Houses of Wood: The Northwest Coast.* Buffalo, N.Y.: Tundra Books, 1992.

Smith, Carter, ed. *Native Americans of the West: A Sourcebook on the American West.* Brookfield, Conn.: Millbrook, 1992.

———. *The Riches of the West.* Brookfield, Conn.: Millbrook, 1992.

White Deer of Autumn. *The Native American Book of Knowledge.* Hillsboro, Ore.: Beyond Words, 1992.

———. *The Native American Book of Life.* Hillsboro, Ore.: Beyond Words, 1992.

INDEX

Italicized page numbers refer to illustrations.

Acorns, 16, 24, *25*, 39
American settlers, 46–49, 51–52
Animal skin blankets, 31

Baking pits, 16
Bartering, 11, 32, 34
Basketmaking, 23, *37*, 39
    present day, 55–56
Baskets, 20, 38, *56*
Bead making, *33*
Beads, 11, 20, 32–34
Blankets, 31
Boat making, 36
Bows and arrows, 23
Buckeye nuts, 24

California Indian tribes, 43

Campsites, 12, 14
Ceremonial houses, *17*
Childbirth, 21
Children, 21, 23, 43
City living, 55
Clamshell beads, 32–34
Clear Lake, *8*, 9, 11
Climate, 12, 14
Clothing, 28–31
Communal houses, 16
Converts, 44
Cooking, 23
    fires for, 16
Cradle basket, *22*
Crafts, 31, 36–39
Currency system, 32, 34, 40
Customs, *53*, *54*, 55

Dances, 43, *53*
Death, 23

Deerskin boots, 31
Diseases, 49, 50
Doctors, 40

Ear ornaments, 36
Education, 55
Epidemics, 49, 50
Extended families, 18

Families, 18, 19-23
Feasts, 18
Fishing, 9, 11, 24, *26*, 27
Fish trading, 9, 11
Food, 24–27, 55
Fort Bragg, 48–49

Ghost dance, 51
Ghost societies, 43
Grandparents, 23
"Great counters," 34

Headdresses, *30*
Healers, 40
Houses, 14, *15*, 16
Hunting, 24, 27

Immunity, 49

"Indian gold," 34

Kashaga, 11
Kelp, 24
Kelsey, Andrew, 46–48
Kin groups, 18
Kuksu cult, 43

Land, 46, 52
Languages, 11, 34, 48, 55

Magnesite, 34
Mantles, 28
Marriage, 19–21
    gifts for, 20–21
Massacres, 51
McKee, Colonel Redick, 48
Meeting hall, 17
Mexico, 46
Money. *See* Currency
Mt. Konocti, *8*

Outfit doctors, 40

Peace, 48
Pomo groups, 11
Population, 49, 51

Prayer rocks, *41, 42*

Rabbit-skin blankets, 21
Rabbit-skin breech-
 clouts, 28
Rancherias, 51–52
Rank in tribe, 18
Redwood forests, 12–14
Reeds, *29*
Religion, 23, 40-43, 55
Religious rituals, 17
Reservations, 51-52
Round Valley
 Reservation, 48
Ruling councils, 18
Russian River valley, 11,
 14, 16

San Rafael mission, 44
Schools, 52
Segregation, 51–52
Shamans, 40
Shoes, 31
Singing doctors, 40
Slavery, 44, 46
Soup, *20*, 21
Spanish missions, 44, *45*

Spawning seasons, 9
Stone, Charles, 46–48
Sucking doctors, 40
Sweathouses, 16–17, 46

Trade, 32-34
Trade feasts, 32
Tribal customs, 23
Tools, 36
Tule, 16, 28, 36

United States Cavalry, 47–48
United States govern-
 ment, 48, 52

Vallejo, Salvador, 46
Villages, 12–18

War, 18, 35
War dances, 35
Waterfowl, 27
Wealth, 31, 34, 39
Weapons, 36
Wedding gifts, 20
White settlers, 44–56
Women, 40, *50*, 55–56
 dress of, 28, 31

[63]

ABOUT THE AUTHOR

Elaine Landau has been a newspaper reporter, a children's book editor, and a youth services librarian. She has written more than sixty books for young people, including *The Sioux*, *The Cherokees*, *The Hopi*, and *The Chilula*. Ms. Landau makes her home in Sparta, New Jersey.